IF ONLY...

Dianne Osborne

PublishAmerica
Baltimore

© 2005 by Dianne Osborne
All rights reserved. No part of this book may be reproduced, stored in a retrieval system or transmitted in any form or by any means without the prior written permission of the publishers, except by a reviewer who may quote brief passages in a review to be printed in a newspaper, magazine or journal.

First printing

At the specific preference of the author, PublishAmerica allowed this work to remain exactly as the author intended, verbatim, without editorial input.

ISBN: 1-4137-9711-3
PUBLISHED BY PUBLISHAMERICA, LLLP
www.publishamerica.com
Baltimore

Printed in the United States of America

To Millie + Lou

Two very wonderful people I'm glad to know.

Dec 7/05

Dianne Osborne

CHAPTER 1

Leo was born with a head of abundant unruly blond hair. Very early in life someone had given him a stuffed lion for Christmas, the only gift he received that year. It had a fuzzy yellow mane similar to his, giving him a sense of false security. He took the toy everywhere and everyone commented on the likeness and soon came to call the child Leo, the Lion.

Many times during his pre-school days his mother—upon rising late in the morning or coming home from the cafe where she waitresses—would tussle his own mane and ask "How's my little Leo, the Lion?"

He thrived on this little bit of attention and would hug her to say thanks. In his little heart he yearned for more of this kind of love but it was not to be. Mother was always either working during the day or out in the evening looking for a better job. Grandma was always with him but she had things to do and when they were done she would read the day old newspaper Mother had brought home from the cafe or else she would sleep in the 'comfort' of the well-worn sofa-chair. At she looked as if she was sleeping.

When he started school it was somewhat better. At least there were kids his own age to play with and the teacher always greeted him pleasantly each day sometimes with a tousle of his hair.

Soon it was his turn for 'show & Tell". There wasn't much at home to bring to show the class or tell about it. Everyone in the cold-water flat where he lived all seemed to like his stuffed lion. "If everyone likes him I'm sure the teacher and the other kids will like him too!"

Off he went that morning with a song in his heart and the stuffed lion tucked under his arm. When it was time to go to the front, he went proudly.

As he started to speak, snickers and twittering came to his ears. He stopped talking not really knowing what to do. "Why are ya bringing a baby toy to school?" "Are you still in diapers?" "Hey he looks like you"

Tears came to Leo's eyes. He recognized the tone of the voices as being unkind, like the voices he had heard from some of the older boys who played in the street where he lived. He was hurt. The teacher settled the class with some difficulty then tried to calm Leo. That too was not easy.

At noon recess the boys and girls started to tease Leo calling out "Leo, the lion! Leo, the lion" in a singsong manner. The teacher saw Leo leave the school grounds but did not call him back. "He needs to be alone" she thought. She understood the feelings of these slum kids from broken homes. She had been one herself.

Leo trudged home with heavy steps, dragging the toy lion by its hind leg. He climbed the three flights of worn carpeted stairs hoping Grandma would be able to give one of her rare hugs. She was 'snoozing' in her chair so he retraced his steps to sit on the cement steps that led to the entrance door of the dirty red brick building he called home.

He sat there all afternoon until his mother came. She had a smile for him and her usual tousle and question to which he answered a dull "Fine". She didn't seem to notice his tone of voice as she went to cook a meal as best she could with what she had. A waitress's pay wasn't very much. She tried to supplement by playing the VLT's but they weren't paying to good lately and neither were the men.

Leo sat till his mother called him for supper. He sat and thought how old he felt for his six year; of how he felt as if the whole world was on his shoulders; of how his friends had been so cruel.

There was so much he couldn't understand. Why did they refer to him as a baby? There was no one around to tell him that child treasures were brought to playschool or kindergarten for 'Show & Tell" but not once you're in grade one. You had to bring something more sophisticated like a computer game! But he hadn't gone to playschool or kindergarten. He didn't even know they existed. His mother, knowing she couldn't financially send him, just never told him about them.

He also couldn't understand how his mother's once loving tousle and pet name was such an irritation to him this afternoon. He knew she would do it and he cringed inwardly when she did. He took it 'like a man' because he didn't want to hurt her feelings.

He really didn't want to go to school the next day but he liked school, he liked the learning, he liked the teacher and he did like the boys and girls before yesterday. So he went and found that the kids were more or less civil to him. Of course, he didn't know the teacher had given them a lesson on manners yesterday afternoon.

CHAPTER 2

School became, over the years, a guessing game. He could always count on a day of learning which he grabbed at with relish. It was the social activities that kept him on his toes. He never knew when the main antagonizer of his crowd would decide it was time for some harassment. Of course, many others joined him in this so-called fun. They were too afraid of the group bully not to.

Frequent trips to the barbershop would have helped a great deal but with a shortage of coin, haircuts were few and far between. Hair gel would have also worked but again finances didn't allow for cosmetics except Mother's lipstick and mascara. Slicking his wild crop of hair down with water only helped until the first recess when his hair dried.

Delving into his books helped him to forget his personal frustration and the teasing that caused it. He became an excellent student scholastically, keeping up with the students from the better classes of society. Of course, socially they had nothing to do with him; unruly hair or no unruly hair, he was from the slums.

As he grew into adolescence his body grew tall and slim. In junior high he tried out for sports and made the basketball team. His agility

IF ONLY...

and great ability to play the game stemmed from the hours of solitary practice on the hoop set up on the vacant lot near his home. Sometimes when the local neighborhood kids, who were also his classmates, were in a good mood, pick-up teams were formed and a summer evening was passed in the challenge of beating the bully's team. Even the threat of more teasing and/or a shove or two, didn't dampen the great feeling Leo felt when the prospect of beating the bully was at hand. It was a great accomplishment when the game was won.

One day as Leo left the school grounds he said his usual 'so longs' and 'see ya laters' to the gang as they dispersed to go their separate ways. He noticed Lisa a few yards ahead of him. She had been with him since grade one and had also changed to the same high school along with the rest of the kids from the neighborhood.

Lisa had always been part of the crowd yet not part of it. She refrained from the teasing and always kept to the rear at the basketball games in the empty lot. There, but not really mingling. She was an average student, not needing any discipline to be directed at her.

Leo knew she lived on his block. He had seen her from time to time but had never paid any attention to the exact building she called home. Maybe that was because she always seemed to be home before he climbed his three flights of stairs.

Today she was late leaving the schoolyard and was walking quite fast as if to make up for lost time. Leo called to her anyway. "Hey, Lisa! Wait up!"

She slowed her pace but did not stop or look anywhere else except where she was placing her feet.

He soon caught up to her matching his pace to hers, "Mind if I walk with you?" he asked.

"No, no, I guess it's okay," she answered in a hesitating manner and without taking her eyes from the sidewalk.

They walked together a short distance which allowed an awkwardness to develop in Leo. "This is just great!" Leo chided himself inwardly. "I've known Lisa all my life! Why can't I think of something to say?"

Corning to the corner, Leo automatically turned left to set himself in the direction of home. Thinking Lisa would do the same, he was surprised when she quietly mumbled, "See ya later, Leo," as she turned right.

"Hey, where ya going?" Leo asked corning out of his self-thoughts.

"Oh, uh, well, uh…I'm going to my aunt's," Lisa finally blurted out.

"Well, can I walk ya there?"

"No" Lisa said flatly

"Oh." Leo was disappointed and tried not to show it as he answered, "Well, okay. I guess I'll see ya tomorrow. Bye." He gave a half-hearted wave and turned into his homeward direction.

Lisa said, "Yeah, see ya tomorrow," and hurried away.

The next day Leo met Lisa in the hallway with a couple of her girl friends. In passing Leo cheerily called out, "Hi girls. Hi Lisa. How's your aunt?"

Lisa answered quietly "Fine," but did not stop to elaborate on the situation. The girl friends followed, one of them saying, "I didn't know you had an aunt!"

The other pitched in, "Where does she live?"

Leo stopped walking while the girls continued on their way. As they left his hearing range, he heard Lisa saying something about "tracks" and "don't want to talk about it".

"Strange," he thought, "Someone not wanting to talk about their aunt. But I guess that's her business." He shrugged his shoulders and continued on his way.

It turned out to be a bad day. The class bully spent noon hour in detention after not having his assignments done even after having been given three extended deadlines

This put him in a bad mood taking his frustration out on Leo who was in dire need of a haircut. The temptation to flatten the bully's fat, pudgy nose was great as Leo fought his way through the crowd of noisy students and slamming locker doors at the close of the day.

It seemed ages before he was able to reach the sanctuary of his front steps. It was odd that a space as open as the front stairs of a rundown neighborhood could be such a comfort to him. But then again when you really thought about it, the snotty-nosed kids played in the alley using

IF ONLY...

the black metal fire escapes as playground bars. Older sisters shouted at them for being so careless when make-believe robbers tipped over the bottle of nail polish the girls were painting their toes with. Old scrawny men and old flabby women shuffled by him on the street with the only thought in their minds was the hope of getting home to relieve themselves of the small shopping bag of groceries that was becoming heavier with each unsteady step. Being mid-week most of the guys his age were at their part-time jobs: janitor at the corner cafe, picking garbage at the park, etc.

So Leo sat in his solitary haven thinking back to a previous bad day about ten years ago when his mother ruffled not only his hair on his head but the hair on the back of his neck.

He sat quietly for a while, his elbows on his knees, hands clasped, head hanging down so the only view he saw was the scuffs on the toes of his shoes. Recognizing the sound of his mother's laugh, he looked in that direction seeing her walking jauntily towards him, her arm entwined in the arm of a man.

"Another boyfriend," Leo thought despondently. "Another evening on my own. But then, what's new?" and he sighed.

"Hello, Leo," she said cheerfully as she started up the steps. For her sake he wanted to reply in the same manner, but before he could speak, the 'dumb jerk' who was with her suddenly reached out his hand and ruffled Leo's hair while saying in a feigned cheerful voice, "Hi there, Leo. Say, that's some mane of hair you've got there! Almost like a lion's."

Leo saw red. He stood up like a spring released. This was not the school ground so he could do something about this remark. Catching the pleading look on his mother's face, he did not move. He towered above and held his trembling clenched fists at his side while menacingly saying through clenched teeth, "Don't you ever touch my hair"

The guy backed down a step holding his hands defensively in front of himself "No, no. I won't. No offense, Buddy. Sorry!" he said as he looked at the woman with him as if to say, "What kind of nut have you got for a son?"

Leo's mother started to put her hand on Leo's arm but thought better of it. Instead she said to her new companion, "Come inside. I'll see if I can fix us something to eat." And they entered the dingy foyer.

Leo sat down in somewhat the same position as before, running his own hand through his hair to push it back. It didn't help his temper any when his hair fell forward again onto his forehead.

Taking both hands he grabbed two fistfuls of hair and tugged. Grinding his teeth he said to whomever wanted to listen "God, how I hate my hair" Surely there is something that can be done with it!"

Elbows on his knees, his head in his hands, he would have cried had it been in his nature to do so. Instead he called on his conscience, his inner-self, the only two friends he ever had. He asked himself questions, Why do I hate my hair? Why am I so touchy about it, so self-conscious about it? Why did I have to be born with this hair? Why? What?

Soon he became calm and began to think rationally. He noticed in the first week or so of a new haircut, the teasing subsided. There was no mane to help remind anyone of his resemblance to a lion. More frequent haircuts would be the answer as was his frequent thought—but not on his newspaper delivery job's wages. Albeit, it had helped but constant short hair, he felt, would probably be the answer.

Where could he get the extra money? There was no use asking his mother. He learned in the early days of his newspaper route that he needn't expect anything from her.

As he sat lost in thought, a little old lady full of wrinkles came and sat down on 'his' steps. She set her shopping bag down with a sigh of relief. "I'm sure the way gets longer every time I go for groceries," she said to no one in particular.

He shared his steps for a few moments before he caught sight of the name of the grocery store on the side of the bag. Slowly an idea took shape. "That's what I'll do!" he said out loud.

The old lady turned around at the sound of his voice and scowled at him. She rose stiffly to her feet, took up her burden and began the rest of her trip home.

"Thank you, Ma'am!" Leo said to her.

She stopped and looked at him. "What're ya thanking me fer?" she asked.

"For giving me life!" Leo replied with a smiling face.

"I ain't your ma!" she croaked and turned away. For the second time that evening he was regarded as being not quite all there.

Leo sat awhile longer while a good feeling crept over him. The evening was moving on; the distant tingling of an untuned piano at the local bar broke the quiet of the streets. His mother and her friend came out and headed in the direction of the music and laughter. He noticed as they exchanged waves of the hand that she had changed clothes.

Suddenly he got up and ran up the stairs to his room. As he grabbed his basketball—one week's newspaper wages—he heard granny snoring. Her daughter had helped her to bed before she left.

After throwing a few balls at the basket in the vacant lot, he came back to his room in the wall—once it was a walk-in closet. Just as unconsciousness took over, he assured himself that from now there'll be nothing but good times!

CHAPTER 3

The interview at the grocery store went well. He had to get a haircut first, and then was told he needed a white shirt, semi-dress pants and shoes, no sneakers. A trip to the thrift store accomplished this but lunch at the canteen was going to be skimpy for the next week.

He worked everyday after school from 4-9 then on Saturdays 9-3. Good hours, good pay, and he still could keep his newspaper route if he wanted.

Saturday morning he turned into an aisle with his cart full of produce to be shelved. In the same aisle Lisa was doing her shopping. She was surprised to see him there. Her cheery "Well, hello!" told him she was pleased with his looks. He knew that the red tie and apron the store supplied set off his white shirt and black pants. His short haircut and comfortable looking shoes finished the good-looking picture.

They chatted a moment before she continued her shopping and he to stock the shelves. When she left the store, he noticed she took the cart with her. It held a small bundle of groceries, light enough—Leo was sure—for even her small frame to be able to carry it the few blocks home. He wondered why she needed the cart!

His wonderment was fulfilled the following Saturday. He was walking to work; the girl he was following was Lisa. She was pushing what he thought was the same grocery cart. When crossing at the intersection she was so careful in handling the cart and at times having difficulties as well. Getting closer he could hear glass tinkling.

"She has that cart full of bottles! She's probably taking them to the bottle depot next to the grocery store!"

Not wanting her to know he was behind her, he slipped into the alley and went into the back door of the store where he was employed. Immediately he went to the front windows and watched from a distance as she entered the bottle depot.

Soon she was in the store with the empty cart. Leo had by this time donned his tie and apron and was 'busy' stocking shelves. When she left the store, he again noticed the small parcel in the big cart. He surmised that the groceries cost close to the amount she had received for the bottles.

No one knew better than Leo what it was like to live in the slums. Hunger was only one part of it. Until he was ten when he started his newspaper route, he missed lunch many times. A glass of milk was a luxury he could afford only periodically. Hanging around with his neighborhood bunch didn't hurt so badly. They were no better off than he was. They all felt the same pangs of empty stomachs as they watched the other kids from the better class homes pass by with hamburgers, fries, coke and sometimes pie. What did pie taste like?

Out of one of his first wages he treated himself to a large milk and a piece of pie.

Everyone wanted a taste so he shared. There wasn't much left for him, but it taught him a lesson. If you are going to flaunt your money, don't do it in front of those who don't have any.

Eventually the rest of the crowd obtained part-time jobs and it became a 'thing' to have milk and pie on paydays. By missing a few milk and pie days he was able to purchase gym clothes and other necessities. Now with the store job he was able to treat those with whom he lived.

He knew he was lucky to have his grandmother with him. She paid the rent from her social security cheque. To show his appreciation, he bought her a small brooch with fake stones in it. He thought she could use it to keep her shawl closed in front.

When he handed it to her, he said "Here. Grandma, this is for you. You've paid the rent all these years, and I wanted you to know how much I appreciate it."

She looked at it then him. "Where'd you get that?" she croaked.

"I've got a better job now so I was able to buy it for you," he said.

"Probably stole it, you mean!" She eyed it a minute then told him, "Put it on my table here beside me. I'll decide later whether I'll accept stolen goods or not." She leaned back and closed her eyes, a sign, Leo knew, of dismissal.

Leo's hurt lasted until a few days later when he noticed her wearing it. The reason she put it on was out of his grasp, and he wasn't going to ask. He also wasn't going to buy her anything else. He did wonder, however, what would happen to his mom and himself if she died.

"I'll cross that bridge when I get to it," he thought to himself. "What I have to worry about now is Lisa."

That thought brought him up short. "Why do I have to worry about Lisa? She's not my sister or even my girlfriend. She means nothing to me. Or does she?" He pondered this for a long time sitting on his steps.

"She's always been my classmate, always my neighbor, always…been there. Yet I've never got to know her! Why? Is it because she's so quiet and so little? Her skinny legs…no, they're slim legs! She hasn't got much up top but it goes well with the rest of her body. In fact, she's got quite a trim figure!" His eyes seemed to widen as this delightful thought came to him. "And her hair! Long, straight, the auburn strands that are parted in the middle framing her tiny facial features looks like its soft to touch! Ummm…."

He sprang to his feet as a thought hit him and hurried up to his room, counted his money and said "Yes, that's enough for us to go to the movies on Saturday night and have pop and popcorn too!"

Leo was able to catch Lisa alone at her locker the next morning. When he asked her for the date he had dreamed about all night, she looked up at him with round, hazel eyes that saw a handsome fellow student wanting nothing more than a pleasant evening out. When she finally said "Yes, Leo. I'd like to go to the movies with you." Leo felt like all the air he was holding in his lungs came out in a great gush when he replied "Great! Pick you up at 8!"

"I'll meet you at the front door steps," she said quietly lowering her eyes and moving on to her classroom.

"Fine by me!" he called back grabbing his gym bag.

How those three days of school dragged. Even Saturday at the store. He was kept really busy but made time to whisper to Lisa in the aisle where she was selecting groceries "See ya tonight!" Her reply was a pleasant smile.

He was ready by 7:30. What to do? "Go sit on your steps like you usually do!" He took an old newspaper to sit on.

Close to 8 o'clock Lisa came shyly out. He wanted to run, but decided that a nonchalant stroll with hands in his pockets would be better. She smiled at him as he neared and he smiled back. "Evenin' Ma'am," he quipped. "Could this humble gentleman offer you his arm to guide you along so you don't trip and break a slender little ankle?"

Lisa laughed and took his arm. Leo laughed and felt good all over. They talked and laughed the whole six blocks to the movie theatre. It was if they had known each other all their lives. They had, really, but their friendship had just begun.

Neither one could tell anyone else what the movie was about so conscious of each other they were. Leo felt great "This is what living is all about!" Reality set in when he noticed Lisa had brought half her pop and popcorn home with her.

The awkwardness returned at the doorstep.

"Thanks.... Thanks for a great time, Leo. It's...well...it's my first date," Lisa stammered.

"Thank you, Lisa, for coming with me. I guess it's been my first real date, too. Uh, do you think we could do it again? Sometime?"

"I...I guess so."

"Great! Well...." He wanted to give her a little kiss on the cheek or maybe on the lips, whichever got in the way but all too soon Lisa was saying "Good-night, Leo. Thanks again." And was letting herself into her own dingy foyer and a couple of flights of worn carpet stairs.

CHAPTER 4

Lisa and Leo were both sixteen years of age when they had their first date. Their sophomore year at school was behind them, their junior year lay ahead. Leo could see nothing but a great time to be had with Lisa as his girl.

As usual the freshman's prom was the first of the round of yearly activities. Leo hated his prom mainly because they had ridiculed him so much about his hair. He realized initiation was a time for joking but he felt that the seniors went overboard while the bully got away with next to nothing. Thinking about it later Leo was able to put two and two together. It came up four when he noticed the bully becoming just a little 'bit more than friendly with the seniors.'

He vowed that when it was his turn to invoke punishment on the freshmen he would be fair. But that would be next year. This year he was going to relax, have fun, and make everyone aware that Lisa and he were a twosome.

The dance went well; the school dance band did a great job. Of course, with parents and teachers chaperoning there was no alcohol. Or was there?

IF ONLY...

As the dance was nearing its end, little Joey from down the street came giggling up to Leo and started to tell what Leo thought was going to be a joke. He really wasn't in the mood for a joke from Joey. Joey's jokes could get a little raw, sometimes. Leo was never sure whether Joey just liked to tell those kind of jokes or he told those jokes to sound big to make up for his 5"4" skinny frame. Whatever the reason Leo also had Lisa to think about. She didn't need to hear such garbage.

However, after listening politely for a few minutes, Leo realized that Joey was having a hard time getting his words out of his mouth because of the giggles that were dominating him.

Joey finally left to join his buddies who were holding up the gym wall near the entrance door. They, too, had the giggles.

Leo put Joey out of his mind. The music was beckoning, and he and Lisa answered the call out to the dance floor.

It was after midnight by the time they reached her brownstone flat. He seemed to have such an awkward time saying goodnight to Lisa. He wanted to kiss her and he thought she wanted that too.

They stood facing each other in the shadow of the entrance doorway. He found it quite natural to raise his hands to her upper arms and pull her close to him. Her hands went to his chest. For a second he thought she was going to push him away so he quickly enveloped her in his arms. Her arms went around his neck; he found her mouth. It was warm, it was eager, and she was kissing him back. Wanting more Leo was disappointed when she pulled back and whispered "Goodnight, Leo. Thanks for a very wonderful time."

"Thank you, Lisa!" He didn't recognize his own voice as he added, "See ya on Monday."

"Yeah." Then she was gone.

He made his way down the street to his own steps. His lips burned, his fingers tingled, and his body yearned for the touch of hers. He needed his sanctuary to calm him, to hold on to the sweetness of the night, the sweetness of Lisa's personal perfume. The staleness of his airless room was the last place he wanted to be.

He wasn't sure how long this heavenly reverie lasted before it was broken by the sounds of clumsy footsteps accompanied by foolish giggles that pressed into his brain revealing them as something he had heard before and not too long in the distant past.

Recognition of Joey's attempt at communication brought Leo back to reality. Not wanting to go inside just yet but not wanting to be seen either, Leo stood up and flattened himself against his own recessed entrance. The shadows hid him as Joey and his pals came staggering down the street trying to make conversation between the snippets of idiotic garble. Leo caught the name of the school janitor then something about glue in the closet.

Leo was against alcohol and drugs. He had seen too much of it at the corner bar, had seen his mother swear and stumble up the stairs when she had so much to drink she couldn't see straight. He thought how degrading she and her companions made themselves. It disgusted him to see the blood-shot and purple-veined enlarged noses of the old 'grubbies' that hung around the park benches and slept in store doorways. It disgusted him to see an attractive women, one who could go somewhere on the social ladder just with her looks, lower herself by lowering the top of her dress. A cackle would escape from the toothless-mouthed cronies whose brains were burned by smoking joints.

He wondered if some of these old reprobates had once been smart at school like Joey was. Chemistry was his specialty with math a close second. He wasn't a bad looking kid, his personality mediocre. The way Leo saw it, someday a girl would find that he was the one for her. Not everyone was perfect. There always seemed to be a partner for almost everyone.

Looking at it in that vein Leo could see Joey doing something stupid just to get attention. But alcohol was not the answer. Alcohol? No, that was not alcohol making these kids act so much out of the ordinary. What, then? After some thought, a light bulb went on in Leo's mind. The school hallways had received new tiles over the summer holidays. The leftover glue would have been stored in the janitor's closet. Joey knew enough about the chemical aspect of the glue to realize that a sniff or two would give him a cheap high, one that could give him just enough confidence to ask a girl to dance. But Joey didn't calculate the intenseness of the chemicals causing him to get a little too carried away.

"He's going to have one doozy of a headache tomorrow morning," Leo thought as he sadly climbed the stairs. "What a rotten end to a wonderful evening!"

Monday morning the halls were buzzing with this rumor and that rumor. Nobody knew for sure what was what. Leo kept his thoughts to himself. Sooner or later all would be revealed.

The bell rang signaling the time to go to classes. The principal of the school came on the intercom. First he congratulated the students on a well organized function held on the weekend and on how well behaved the students were. Then his voice changed from cheerfulness to disgust as he vented his anger against alcohol, drugs, and other brain destroying substances. He calmed down enough to inform the students, "Criminal acts must be punished. The instigator of Friday evening escapade has been expelled from school, his innocent victims suspended for two weeks and the janitor has been fired. I'm happy to say, however, that over three quarters of the students of this school have a higher standard of living so as to keep them out of the dregs of society. Have a good day!"

Everyone's breath was let out at once, a murmur swept through the room; the teacher immediately attended to the day's lessons squashing an opinionated discussion that was sure to follow.

Leo would have liked to talk things over with Lisa as they walked home together, but he knew that was out of the question.

Lisa made her rounds each day—Leo found out discreetly—of the of the haunts of the lowly and not so lowly. Down by the tracks there were a number of well-hidden alcoves in the bushes and trees that grew there. Many a lonely soul would drown their sorrows there. Many an executive and their secretaries took part in extra curricular activities there. Many a bottle was left for Lisa to find. Leo knew this, understood, and kept quiet about it to save her embarrassment. He never let on that he knew that there really wasn't an aunt living down by the tracks.

So on Sunday afternoons they took their weekly walk through the park. Sometimes they would sit on one of the benches. It was general knowledge that these benches provided beds for the homeless. As dawn crept through the city, the authorities made sure the benches were clear of their nighttime inhabitants.

Sometimes Leo and Lisa would sit on the banks of the small river flowing through the park. This was their shared sanctuary.

They discussed school, work, Joey and drugs. At least Leo did. Lisa never said much at anytime. He began to wonder if she understood what he was saying or did she even have an opinion of the subject at hand. An odd "That's good!" or "I'm glad you feel that way, Leo," or "I guess so," fell from her lips but not much else. Leo quite frequently wished she would speak more but didn't push the issue. That was Lisa's way. She had many other good qualities about her that had him scrambling for her attention. He did wish, however, that she would talk more about her family.

The scandal of the freshman's prom died down, not forgotten but put on the back burner as Christmas rolled around.

Leo bought a dress and a pair of heeled sandals from the thrift shop for Lisa. When he saw her with her threadbare coat he chided himself for not buying the coat he had found there. It was only $5.00! Oh, well maybe next pay cheque. If it's still there.

Then he noticed her bare toes peeping out from under the long skirt of the dress. "Why didn't I think of that?"

Lisa wondered why they were stopping at the all-night drug store. In a moment Leo was handing her a pair of panty hose. "Here, go put them on in the ladies washroom," he told her.

Coming out to join him Lisa said "Thank you, Leo You think of everything."

"I want my girl to have everything!"

He kissed her forehead. Arm in arm they continued on to the school for the New Year's Eve bash.

Winter left and spring came. Evening basketball games in the empty lot still continued. As new kids joined the ranks, Leo tried to make them feel welcome. Those he could see would make good basketball players were given tips on dribbling or shooting or whatever the downfall was.

The younger ones looked up to Leo. Many were the times they came to him with complaints about the bully. Leo tried to calm their fears but it was difficult especially since he had his own complaints about the antagonizer.

Leo was classified as one of the nice guys in the neighborhood. Although he mostly kept to himself—minding his own business—he was eager to help if asked. When it came to the facts of life, even at his young age, Leo was not naive. Unintentionally his mother's many boyfriends had taught him lots. There were girls in the neighborhood that would allow him freedoms that he didn't want to take with Lisa.

Lisa was his idea of a perfect wife of a middle-income husband who would bear him a couple of kids. They would have a nice home and do all the right things. To kiss Lisa or to hold her was a special thing. She was handled with tender loving care. He put her on a pedestal.

Cohorting with the local neighborhood girls was getting just a little too close for comfort. Flirting was one thing but what he had in mind was another. Being a big kid he surmised that his size would get him into the bars on the other side of town where no one knew him. And there was always free stuff—he was willing to pay for it if necessary—in every section of the city.

When his young hot blood began to flow, a quick trip on the transit bus would find him saddling up to a strange bar looking for strange women. It was the women who usually found him. They loved to run their fingers through his thick blond locks. They loved to feel the muscles in his young arms and chest. It wasn't long before the invitation was voiced with Leo eagerly accepting.

Waking up the next morning in a little fancier flat than his own, he would look at the woman beside him and think, "Who the hell is she? What the hell am I doing here?"

Finding his clothes that had been thrown this way and that the night before, he would quietly slip out and go home to his steps. Here it was that he realized, "Yes, I am definitely the son of the woman I call Mother"

He would justify his actions by telling himself, "I'm practicing for Lisa. I want that girl and when I take her, everything is going to be perfect."

The 'perfect' evening came that fall. They had just started their senior year together, the freshman's prom just on the horizon.

"I saw Joey the other day," Leo told Lisa as they sat near the banks of the river. The day had been hot. The leafy bushes along the shore afforded a cool shelter in which to while away their Sunday evening.

"Oh?" Lisa answered. "I haven't seen him for a long time."

"You don't want to see him! He's just skin and bone. He's taken up smoking, and I don't mean just cigarettes. The sickening sweet odor of his joint just about gave me a high smelling it. I don't think he was too happy to see me. He gave me a dirty look as if it was my fault for the state he was in. Lisa, I bet it won't be long before he's on to something bigger. The long deep drags he was taking gave me the impression he wasn't getting the high he wanted. I won't be a bit surprised if he takes to the needle. Then..."

Lisa laid a small slender hand on his arm saying "Please...sorry if I offended you. I just thought...Leo, don't talk so much. You're wasting a beautiful moon!"

It took only a second for Leo to see which way the wind was blowing—so to speak. Putting his arm around her shoulder he whispered in her ear, "You're so right!"

An embrace, a kiss, and they lay side by side on the lush green of the park lawn.

As he caressed Lisa, his 'justifiable practice' idea never entered his mind. His gentleness with her was as natural as the moon that brightened the night. He knew in his heart that Lisa would be the one by his side through eternity. Taking her on this night of all heavenly nights was the right and perfect thing to do.

Lisa didn't utter a sound even when he knew she was hurting. Only her wet cheeks gave her feelings away. After it was all over, she clung to him. Only the promise of a repeat performance the next night did she consent to let go of him so they could walk home.

There was no awkwardness as he left her at her door. Leo was on a high that no drug or glue sniffing could supply. Her arms, tightly wrapped around his neck told him she was right along with him. Finally, Lisa broke loose and sobbed "Oh, Leo! I don't want to leave you but I have to." And she disappeared into the dimly lit foyer of her shabby home.

By this time in their relationship, Leo had found out that her apartment window on the second floor faced the street. He crossed the street and looked up hoping she might come to the window. He watched as the black glass turned yellow showing a bit of the once white cupboards.

Suddenly the warm night was turning his blood to ice water. He closed his eyes thinking that he had already reached home and was having a bad dream. But when he opened them again the horrible scene was still there.

Lisa was preparing a syringe!

CHAPTER 5

Lisa! Lisa! The name exploded in his mind. The noise in his head caused him to reel and stumble. He groped for his steps. The steps seemed to crumble beneath his weight, the safety gone from them. Blindly and in the darkest of dark tunnels he crawled, he stumbled; he grappled at the steps until he reached the 'comfort' of his stuffy room. He found the bed, tossed, and turned on it stopping only when the two blankets wrapped around him, holding him fast. Exhausted, he lay heaving great sobs from his young broken heart. His face, his hair, and his body were wet with tears and sweat. The natural darkness of the night, his room, and of the situation enveloped his body that was hot and cold at the same time.

Somewhere in the far distance in space and time he heard the kitchen door slam. Foul language came from his mother's mouth as she bumped into furniture making her way to the sofa. She collapsed upon it venting out frustration "The dumb prick! He doesn't know his asshole from a hole in the ground!" Then silence as the alcohol dulled her senses.

Time stopped for Leo. He lay still, calming himself. Thoughts and questions wondered in and out of his mind. Memories reminded him that every time he got onto the subject of drugs and his abhorrent hate of them, Lisa never agreed or disagreed with him. In fact, she would sit there patiently until his frustration was spent then quietly say, "Could we talk about something else?" Of course he would change the subject thinking that maybe girls don't have the same views as guys, nothing else ever entered his mind.

And tonight—it seemed ages ago that he was holding her in his arms experiencing life in all its glory—she just reminded him quietly of a moon that was being wasted. Thinking it was love she wanted and not talk, he obliged her. Was it to steer him away from the possibility of him finding out her secret?

He could not accept the fact Lisa was on drugs. But she did wear quite a few clothes with long sleeves. That was because she was so thin and always cold—right?

Maybe if he talked to her. Maybe she would come clean with him. Maybe he could help her beat the habit. Maybe…

The 'maybes' stirred him to action. Untangling himself from the bedclothes he left the apartment. Reaching his steps he looked her kitchen window. The yellow glass had turned to black again.

"Damn! I'd better not go now. Whoever she's living with doesn't need this kind of interruption."

What to do? No use going back up. Sleep was not for him on this night, this night of horrors, of disbelief, of heartache, of being let down, of….

He started to walk down the street, away from his snoring mother and grandmother, away from his dingy room, away from his school—the epitome of his strength, from Lisa—the light of his life.

An empty streetcar slowed at a regular stop and he hopped on, took a seat at the back, and rode to the end of the line. He continued on in this trance until the milkman started his rounds, the streetlights went out and the store awnings were rolled out.

He took a look around discovering he was in a part of the city he had never been before. It was rather a pleasant piece of urbanization. The more he looked the warmer he began to feel. Contentment stole into his body lighting a light in his mind.

"An excellent idea! Nobody knows me here. I should be able to get a job at a grocery store. I have a résumé now. Just like all working people, like merchants, lawyers, and teachers!

Teachers! This thought brought him up short. School was, for him, a place where the world began. If you didn't have an education you were nothing. Here he was a senior, one more year and he would have his diploma, his ticket to the work place, his ticket to a nice home, a wife....

Lisa was going to be his wife. He had that planned for quite sometime now. The traumatic heaviness of the last few hours finally took its toll. His heart broke. He began to run—where he didn't know. The wind he created pushed his tears on either side of his face where they ran down beside his ears.

He came across a large park. It was midmorning. A few elderly people were sitting on benches soaking up the sun. He found his own bench in a secluded spot and flopped down on it exhausted. He had run a long way, his good physical shape allowed it but frustration and a sleepless night caught up with him.

His troubled mind would not let him rest. He sat until he could breathe easy again. Now he had a headache! His growling stomach told him that food would solve those two minor problems.

A fast foods joint provided a hamburger and a corner lamppost provided companionship while he wolfed down the sawdust and bun.

Once again as he watched the middle classed citizens on parade, a bit of a peace came over him. This was a better section of the city than he was used to. He made up his mind then and there that he was going to get used to it.

"As long as I don't think about Lisa, I'll be alright. What's the next best thing to her?"

A bookstore down the street told him 'school ".

But his weary body told him he needed sleep more than anything else.

He didn't have much money on him. Another streetcar ride took him into the outskirts of the suburbs to a cheap but still half decent hotel.

IF ONLY...

Relocking his room door he flopped on the bed. Sweet sleep took away his cares and woes.

When he awoke it was dark. Confusion reigned. Switching on the bedside lamp he looked at his watch that said it was late evening. The strange room and strange neon lights outside his window brought him back to the present and confusion left.

A quick shower freshened him. Propped up on the pillows he could watch the blink-blink of the sign across the street, while still in the seclusion of the darkened room. He could have opened the window for air, something he had never had the privilege of doing but he didn't want the noise of the traffic. He liked the quiet. He liked the feel of clean cotton sheets and fluffy pillows; he liked the sight of scenic pictures on the walls and plush carpet on the floors. Again he had that feeling that things were going to be good again.

"As long as I don't think of Lisa!"

A week later Leo was back in his old neighborhood, not because he wanted to be there but because he had to be there. A school in his new location had accepted him; a call to his former boss landed him a job at another store of the same chain. A small partially furnished apartment was another accomplishment of the past week.

He went to his old school just at a time when he knew Lisa would already be down at the tracks, at a time when 90% of the students would be gone. He came to clean out his locker, to retrieve his gym bag, shoes, papers, etc.

Mixed emotions filled Leo as he walked the empty halls for the last time. When he neared his locker he recognized one of his few close friends that he had.

A surprised look crossed over the friends face when he saw Leo coming towards him, then happiness and excitement took over.

"Hey, Leo! Hey, man! Great to see ya! Where ya been?"

They shook hands and patted each other on the back. "Oh, I've been busy doing things. And it's great to see you too!" Leo answered.

"We've all missed you here, Leo. Especially Lisa. She's sure down in the mouth. Hey, you guys split up or something?"

Leo had started stuffing items into his gym bag, his head half in the locker. He closed his eyes and spoke in as natural voice as possible. "Uh, I'd rather not talk about it right now, ok, Pal?"

"Yeah, sure. Whatever you say. Not a problem. Hey, I don't suppose you heard about Joey."

"No, what about Joey?"

"Last Monday, real early in the morning, a night cop found his body in the alley behind the corner pub. Story goes he ODed on crack. Seems he died Sunday evening."

Leo's blood ran cold. He slowly turned to look at his pal. In disbelief he said, "You're not kiddin' me?"

"Wish I was. Seems that after he was expelled after that glue caper last freshman's prom, he just lost his cool. Started smokin' cigs then went onto joints. It wasn't long before he needed something else stronger to keep him going."

Silence filled their space. Leo couldn't think of anything to say, neither could his friend. Shuffling awkwardly from one foot to another, the friend finally said, "Well, I guess I'll see ya around. Sorry I had to tell you such bad news." And he was gone.

Numbly Leo finished emptying his locker and slowly left. Numbly he climbed the stairs to his mother's apartment and finished filling his gym bag with the rest of his few belongings.

On his way out he left a note: "Bye, Mom. Bye, Grandma." and signed his name.

Entering into his old street he turned towards the streetcar stop, which was in the opposite direction of Lisa's home. He wanted to look at the window but decided he would probably hurt too much. He didn't stop to think that maybe Lisa's heart would be broken as she watched him walk down the street and into the bus with his gym bag clutched in his hands. Tears freely flowed as she watched him walk out of her life. Why? It was beyond her comprehension.

Leo reached his new abode and emptied his bag. There was a great deal yet to do to make this home but he had all the time in the world.

He placed his things in the drawers. When he came across Lisa's picture that he just about left behind, he sat down on the bed and stared at it.

IF ONLY...

So many things went through his mind. All good things. But drugs got in the way. Look at Joey!

Tears began to fall as he realized "Joey died that night, that same night that Lisa experienced life for the first time but threw it away so soon after. Lisa may as well have joined Joey!"

He put her picture in the bottom of the drawer. Maybe someday when he had come to terms with her "death" he's take it out again.

CHAPTER 6

Life goes on after a death, whether it is a real or superficial death. Adjustments are made. For some it is difficult to make the transition, for others acceptance takes over making the daily chores easier. Even though Leo's heart was heavy he knew he had to be strong and carry on. But why? Who was there that would care whether or not he was eating, sleeping, working or playing, hating or loving? In the last ten years since he left the sanctuary of his steps he had heard only once from his Mother. She had traced him down to let him know grandma had died.

He was polite to her and offered his condolences. There would be no funeral; finances didn't allow it. Leo wasn't sure if the mention of finances was a subtle probe into his affairs so he offered no information, nor did he inquire of hers. The conversation was soon cut short.

Just before Monica came to live with him Leo had moved to a bigger and better apartment, which he had furnished himself in a plain decor. He was proud of it and he was proud of his small climb up the social ladder. His ticket to the work world had been obtained from the school in the area and his work experience at the store had warranted him a higher position, a higher wage and the attention of one of the manager's daughters.

After a couple of years together Monica became dissatisfied with the simplicity of their residence and was constantly nagging Leo for better accommodations.

The apartment wasn't the only item of dissension that caused their break-up. His great desire to help girls on drugs or to keep them off them made for much jealousy on Monica's part.

When she left, Leo had sat himself down to analyze the whole situation. There were no steps for his contemplation, just a comfortable armchair with a small table beside it that held a lamp, the TV remote control, ashtray and his cigarettes. He felt no remorse. She had filled a need but not the empty spot. He was glad to be on his own again.

Being on one's own means being independent. Leo was that in many ways. He kept a clean house and a well-stocked cupboard that provided him not only simple meals when he was in a hurry but a few experimental gourmet dishes on a lazy Sunday afternoon or day-off. His only two dependences were on the city transit system to get him to work and to the easy girls at the bar for 'temporary' love.

On this night his need for a woman was greater than it had been for a long time. Was it because his regulars hadn't been too regular lately? Was it because his regular habits with Monica had been such a long time ago?

The thought of Monica brought other things to mind. Why was she so dissatisfied with his humble home? Was it because her parents had been able to provide her with better? She often complained about the second hand furniture even though the new items blended in well with the still sturdy older pieces. Maybe it was because of her social status that she wanted more. He didn't know but he knew in his heart that had Lisa been with him, she would feel as if she was living in a palace.

Lisa! His heart lunged at the mere thought of her. Where was she? At that moment he had such a strong urge to hold her in his arms, to feel again her slim body next to his, her lips burning into his. But where would he find her—at home? At a rehab center? In jail? These thoughts made him sick at heart.

He went into his bedroom to his dresser and slowly opened the bottom drawer. His trembling fingers found the age old school picture of his dream girl. Slowly he drew it out and gazed again at the long straight reddish tresses framing a pixie face devoid of any make up. She didn't need it. Hers was a soft complexion, her fair lashes and eyebrows enhanced the hazel eyes that in the bright sunshine appeared green.

It was fortunate the picture was in a frame. His trembling, his yearning to hold her tight, was such that he would have crushed it.

Instead he held the frame close to his chest, flopped on the bed on his back and cried like a baby. Tears rolled into his ears. He rolled over to wipe them on his pillow still firmly holding the frame to his chest.

Blessed sleep partially comforted him intermittently through the night with heartache and agony being his other "comforters."

He was exhausted when the sun finally peeped through his window as it rose over the square and steepled horizon. Through the day he kept Lisa with him—on the fridge, by the lamp. By the time evening came his physical desire for a woman rose again. A picture, although it can satisfy in many ways is still only a piece of paper. He needed flesh.

He set Lisa's picture on his night table where he could see it at dawn's first light. He shrugged on a hooded fleece, blew Lisa a kiss and promised "I'll be back." then left the apartment to look for that much needed flesh.

Entering his usual drinking hole he noticed only a very few patrons. Not surprising, it was still early. He ordered a draft, chatted with the bartender and impatiently waited on the barstool

After awhile he felt a small hand on his shoulder. For the past twenty-four hours Lisa had been "with him" so close in spirit that his heart flipped, his sub-conscious taking over.

He turned to see who belonged to the hand. Disappointment showed in every line of his face. But Stephie didn't notice. She was one of those "dumb blondes" camouflaged. Her hair was dyed jet black, black mascara and eyeliner stood out starkly in her white face accented with next-to-black lipstick. She wore black clothing to contrast with her pale skin of which a great deal was showing.

"Why" Leo thought, "do hefty girls always wear scanty clothing that

IF ONLY...

not only show off their big boobs but their rolls of fat as well?" He shuddered to think he had been desperate enough to take her to bed.

Stephie was all smiles and googly-eyed as she hefted herself up on to the bar stool next to Leo.

"Hi, Leo, you good lookin' man, you. Gonna buy me a drink?"

Quietly and grudgingly Leo reached into his pocket and threw a two-dollar coin on the counter motioning the bartender to bring her a beer.

"Thanks, Leo. How ya been doing? Haven't seen you lately. Where ya been?"

"I've been working" was all Leo could say before diverting his eyes elsewhere in hopes she either would stop talking or go away. He was looking for flesh but not that much.

The black-haired blonde did neither. Not wanting to be rude, Leo finally got up and said, "I've got to be going" and left Stephie in the middle of her sentence.

Another one of his haunts down the street wasn't any busier. He did see one of his regular girlfriends but she was hanging on to the arm of an older fellow. "Must be short of cash" Leo thought, had a drink and left.

After a number of hours Leo realized in his drunken stupor that he was losing the desire of the flesh. He also realized he had wanted only one particular slim girl. He had encountered a few in the course of the evening but all had the wrong face.

It was past midnight when Leo ordered another drink and was refused. Blearily he eyed the bar tender and noticed there were two of them. 'Surely one of them will give me another drink" came the from Leo's fuzzy brain. So he asked again "Bring me another whiskey."

Both bartenders said simultaneously "I'm sorry, Leo. You've had enough. I can't bring you another drink."

This did not sit very well with Leo's, by now, very irritable disposition. He wasn't in the best of moods when he started his search—just what was his search? Many drinks and many bars later didn't help matters.

"Fuck you, you dumb bastard!" Leo exploded saluting him with his middle finger.

The man behind the bar knew enough not to get upset. He had worked at serving drunks long enough to know to let them say what they wanted. He watched Leo slither off of his stool and run into a chair standing by a table.

"God-damn chair! It wasn't there before!"

He also heard Leo mumble, "Jesus Christ, they don't make doors as wide as they used to!" when Leo struggled to get through the doorway. Leo was the last to leave that bar. The manager locked the door Leo had just passed through. Through the glass he noticed Leo holding up the street post and mumbling incoherently.

When the sidewalk no longer heaved like the ocean, Leo felt he could brave the storm and walk home – wherever home was.

As he staggered in the semi-light of neon and streetlights, he became tired and unsure of himself. He grabbed another lamppost, hung on and tried to get his bearings. The storefronts and office buildings were unfamiliar. Slowly the fog cleared ever so slightly from his brain, just enough to tell him he was far from home. Hanging on to the lamppost with one hand and checking his pockets with the other only made things worse. There was little or no coin for a taxi.

Hanging on to his only friend at the moment while trying to settle the sidewalk again, he spied a recessed door way. His knees were beginning to "give out. "I hope I can make it there."

Reaching the doorway that seemed miles away, he leaned his back against it just before his knees buckled. Once he had accomplished the slide down the door allowing his butt to touch pavement, he sighed a sigh of relief, of hopelessness, of self-pity and closed his eyes. The laxness of his body caused by sleep caused him to fall over sideways.

There he lay until dull jabs to his hips and ribs prompted him to open at least one eye. The polished toe of a black boot topped with a yellow accented blue pant leg popped the other eye open.

Half turning so as to be able to see the whole of the bent over figure, he came face to face with the "bully"

CHAPTER 7

If a bystander had been present watching the cop trying to rouse the drunk he would not have been able to testify as to which one of the two men were more surprised.

Leo struggled to sit upright; the bully, with hands on knees, leaned over further to get a better look at the drunk's face. Both sets of eyes were large; both jaws dropped leaving gaping holes in the faces of the two stunned actors.

Both found their tongues at the same time.

"Leo!"

"Stan!"

"Here, Buddy! Let me help you up" Stan said as he firmly but gently took hold of Leo's arm. Leo was glad of the firm grip and when his feet were finally planted squarely on the doorway pavement, he hung on to Stan's arm and said "Thanks, Pal!"

For a few moments they stood hanging on to each other, looking into each other's face with disbelief that they should be glad to see each other, glad to be together in the cold gray dawn of autumn, away from the slums yet still part of a life they both grew up in. Stan forgot about

Leo's unruly hair, Leo forgot about Stan's irritation when the bully lost the Friday night basketball game in the empty lot. Just to see someone from the past, a past that wasn't as good as the present. Just to see an old school classmate who had basically the same memories as you. Just to see someone you knew, a familiar face out of all the strange ones.

Then they were hugging each other—a burly cop who fought back tears; a skinny, gangly drunk letting the tears flow.

Stan's training brought him around to the business at hand. Untangling himself from Leo's grasp he said, "Leo, I'm sorry to have to break this up but I do have a duty to perform. I should be giving you a ticket for drunkenness in a public place, loitering, etc. but for old times sake I'm not going to. I'm on this beat on foot and alone so I can waiver the ticket without having to explain to a partner. We now need to get you home. Where do you live?"

Leo stood alone or as best as he could and tried to think sensibly. He fumbled in his pockets and brought out his wallet, handed it to Stan and said, "I'm not in my own neighborhood. I'm not sure how to get home. There's my address on my ID card."

"Mmmm... You're not really that far away but too far to walk. Shall I get you a cab?"

"That would be nice but I haven't any cash on me. Maybe just point me in the right direction. I'll get there sooner or later."

"I can't let you do that, Leo. You're not that steady on your pins. Some other cop may stop you and he won't be so lenient. I'll lend you the few bucks for a cab."

Leo started to say "no" but Stan insisted. I'll be around to collect one of these days. I know where you live now. I'll come for a visit and we can talk over the old times."

Stan had no problem calling a cab off the street. Stores were opening; shoppers were appearing now that the transit system had unloaded the office workers. Leo shook Stan's hand as he stumbled into the back seat of the car. Stan gave Leo his wallet back while giving directions to the cabbie. They both waved as the taxi moved out into the traffic.

Leo was a different man when he went to work that week. He blew

IF ONLY...

Lisa a kiss before leaving—to know she would be still there when he came home comforted him. He waved to the cop on his neighborhood beat, he hummed and felt light headed—not from alcohol but from having the knowledge that life really is good. It's all in how you handle it.

It wasn't long before a knock came on his door on a Sunday morning. He was making coffee when he opened the door to find Stan standing there with a six-pack of beer in his hand.

"Hey, Stan! Come in. Come in. Great to see ya!"

"Thanks, Leo" Stan said as he stepped into an apartment that smelled and looked like home. Thinking that Leo was a habitual drunk he pictured a disheveled and dirty flat with little or no food. In a glance he took in the carton of eggs and package of bacon near the stove. The toaster popped up two pieces of brown bread toast.

"Oh, the toast is up. Excuse me while I butter it. May I make some for you too?" Stan noticed Leo was using real butter not margarine before he answered hesitantly "Uh, oh. Well, I guess I can handle a couple of pieces. Thanks." He began to relax causing him to venture a little further "that coffee sure smells good! ""Yeah, nothing like coffee first thing in the morning. Here, I'll get you a cup. Have a chair there at the table. How many eggs do you want?"

"Oh, uh, Two, I guess. Thanks!"

"Easy over?" Leo asked

"Yeah. Actually I've had breakfast a couple of hours ago but you make it sound so pleasant that I can't refuse!" Stan said as he took the offered chair by the table that had a small vase of artificial flowers as a centerpiece.

They exchanged smiles and thumbs up as Leo went about the business of making breakfast for the two of them. You couldn't call them enemies of the past, antagonizers would be more the word but due to time, age and circumstances a friendship that would last through to eternity was forming.

Amiable conversation passed across the top of the small table as well as much catching up of lives. Stan had married a nice girl. She gave him two boys to be proud of.

"You know, Leo, in my bullying days at school I probably inflicted a lot of pain of various kinds. But I never thought by having a little fun with my woman that I would cause her pain enough for everyone I bullied. When she gave birth to those two boys she went through hell. So much so I was beginning to feel bad about the whole issue. Can you imagine, me, the bully of the neighborhood, feeling bad about somebody being hurt?"

"No. I truly can't" Leo answered with a chuckle causing both to break out in laughter. Underneath Leo felt a slight twinge of pain or maybe it was envy. To experience the role of fatherhood seemed to be an illusion that kept fading away. He could even see it never happening to him and it bothered him in an odd sort of way.

Wanting to change the subject Leo asked Stan if he'd like to see the apartment. "The place was too plain for Monica. Let's get your opinion" Leo quipped.

As soon as Leo walked into the bedroom he knew he had made a mistake. It was so natural and normal to see Lisa's picture beside the bed he never thought that questions may be asked if someone else saw it. But who ever saw his bedroom? He was just trying to get personal subjects out the window by turning attention to apartments.

"Maybe I can reach it and discretely lay it down," thought Leo. Too late. Stan was exclaiming "Hey that's Lisa, isn't it? Do you see her often?"

"Yes, that's Lisa and no, I haven't seen her since the day Joey ODed."

"Hey, that was messy wasn't it? Look at you and me. We're both from the slums and we've done fairly well for ourselves. Joey could be the same as us, not doing extremely well and then maybe yes, he could be doing extremely well, cause Joey had the smarts. But I think ol' Schneider went just a little too far in his punishment, don't you?"

Leo only had time to nod in the affirmative as Stan was continuing….

"A week's suspension would have been plenty. Like I said, Joey had the smarts. He could have caught up easily then gone on to graduate with the rest of us. Hey, speaking of graduation, we sure missed you! "

IF ONLY...

A lump came to Leo's throat when he thought of his lonely graduation ceremonies. He didn't go to the prom; he was still too hurt.

"Yeah, I missed you guys too! Sitting with all those strangers who had so much in common, I felt a little out of place. But I was glad I was there. Did, uh, did Lisa make it okay?"

"No. Lisa dropped out of school a couple of months after you left. She never was a real brain but was still able to keep her head above water. That is until after you left. She just kind of went to pieces and quit. I haven't seen her since. Hey, what happened there? You guys were such a happy twosome for a couple of years."

Leo fidgeted inside himself. Should he be taking Stan into his confidences. It would be nice to talk about it with someone; maybe they could offer some insight into the whole mess. Then again, they might be blabbermouths too. He decided to keep it to himself so he told Stan "Well, it's a long story, Stan. I'd rather not get into it right now."

"Hey, Buddy, that's fair. It's none of business anyway."

Leo thought he saw a bit of disappointment in Stan's face as if he was missing out on some juicy gossip. "I'm glad I didn't tell him," Leo thought. Out loud he said, "How about sampling that beer you brought. We could sit with our feet up and solve all the world's problems."

They sat with their feet up sipping their beer and a world problem did come up in their conversation. A surprise to both of them was that they both had an adamant hatred for drugs.

"I know I get drunk on alcohol and do some stupid things. I also know alcohol can be addictive and unhealthy for your body. And alcohol can also lead to drug abuse. You have to learn to know your limits. I guess I should practice what I preach. When you found me I was over my limit just a little too much."

They both chuckled over this as both remembered their unusual reunion.

They tossed the drug issue around and found that they both were active in the youth drug preventative programs. This news warranted a healthy handshake. The day wore on until Stan realized he had better get home. "Leo, I have to confess to you that after seeing you in the doorway I thought you had fallen along way down into the dregs of society. My intentions in coming here today were to try to make you see what harm you were doing to yourself. I admit that I am more than pleased to see you with your head squarely on your shoulders. Hey, what if it does get knocked off once in a while, you know how to put it back on right. You've got a nice place here, simple but clean. Your hospitality is great and your heart is big and warm. Buddy, I'm glad to know you, then and now!"

They shook hands, hugged, then said their 'so Longs" just like at the gate of the schoolyard. They both knew they would see more of each other when busy schedules allowed.

CHAPTER 8

    Leo was reaching thirty years of age. Still a very young man in mind and spirit, still full of energy that was needed at the store he now managed; still capable of scoring baskets at the Thursday night adult basketball club which Stan had also joined.
    The club members were always thoroughly entertained when Stan and Leo were captains of opposing teams. The old personal antagonism showed through giving any spectator a show of their life. No matter who won there was no animosity, only a hearty shake of the hand, a few slaps on the back and a smiling "Great game!" was verbally exchanged.
    Leo and Stan saw each other periodically at drug prevention meetings. They also attended a conference or two together once traveling to another city, an experience in itself being that both men had never left their home city before. And the friendship blossomed. Stan would invite Leo over for a Sunday dinner once in awhile encouraging Leo to bring a lady friend, which he did sometimes. While there Leo could see in the elaborate decor of the house and yard Stan's penchant for prestige and glamour. The school days attitude of "I am somebody!" showed through in his house and family.

Financially Stan and Leo were more or less on the same level.

Leo respected Stan for his lavishness—that was Stan's personality. Stan returned that respect for Leo's simple, humble style of living. Leo could have a fancy home but with no one to build it for, he was content in his plain apartment. He steered his interests into helping others fight the drug habit and trying to curb his own bad habits.

He knew he was his mother's son, that someday he would go on another binge such as the one when Stan found him. He knew it and it scared him. Stan was his savior once but it may not be that way again.

It was going on two or three years since Stan and Leo's reunion. Leo noticed he had to fight the urge to "let go." Lisa's picture helped somewhat although thoughts of "what does it matter. She may be in jail or even dead from an over dose!" ran through his head.

Leo was capable of going to the local bar and having a few drinks before returning home at a respectable hour. So when the heavy inebriation set in it was not a planned event.

His visit to the bar started out like any other visit. Looking around as he entered he saw a few people he knew but chose to sit by himself at the bar. He and the bartender were sometimes able to get into some good conversations, depending on the number of patrons present.

As he slowly drank his draft beer, a man joined him, about his own age, where upon they began to converse on general subjects when the topic of dope came to the surface.

Leo was always on the lookout for new members for the drug prevention society he and Stan belonged to. The more he talked to this stranger, the more the stranger became animated in what Leo believed to be a strong feeling for anti-drugs for young girls. Drugged teens became teen prostitutes, some of them dead prostitutes. This pricked Leo's heart to the core; this was his own pet peeve. This newfound acquaintance was singing the same tune Leo was. Leo became excited and willingly went along with the suggestion of his "friend".

"Hey, I have an idea!" said the stranger/friend. "I know a few young teen girls who hang out in the next district. Why don't we go have a friendly chat with them to see if we can do something for them? There's quite a gang of girls and guys who keep the chairs warm at a licensed

IF ONLY...

cafe. We can still have a beer or two while we try some anti-drug persuasion on them."

The two eager "drug preventers" boarded a streetcar arriving shortly at the aforesaid cafe.

The streetlights were on full force when the stranger was heartily welcomed by the young crowd. Leo was introduced and only half-heartily welcomed. Street gangs are always leery of newcomers until he/she has proven himself. An older person entering into their territory could be outright dangerous. An invitation to a pop by their older friend set them somewhat at ease and they all trooped inside, found a couple of tables to pull together whereupon they sat to cheerily gab and sip.

Leo followed in the rear surveying the fourteen to seventeen year olds. His eyes fell on a young long blonde haired girl "About 15" Leo thought. She made his heart skip a beat—her hair was worn just like Lisa had worn hers. But it wasn't so much her hair—many girls wore it that way—but her big blue eyes bothered him. They looked so familiar yet he couldn't place them.

With difficulty he put his own thoughts and feelings away to concentrate on the business at hand—that of subtly warning these beautiful kids of the danger of drugs.

To make matters worse this blue eyed, twiggy blonde took a shine to Leo choosing to sit beside him to frequently give him a glance and a smile. The smile, after a couple of glasses of cola turned to a giggle. Leo also noticed the others getting quite giggly as well.

Some were rolling roll-your-owns. Experience told Leo there probably was more than tobacco in those cigarettes.

Leo leaned forward putting his elbows on the table and his head between his hands, letting his fingers run into his hair that was overdue for a haircut.

'Something is wrong with this picture!' He began to chide himself "I've had too much to drink to be effective. I had too much before I got here, these kids aren't going to listen to a drunk!"

He nudged his new friend and whispered "I don't think we will be able to get through to these kids if we're half pissed ourselves!"

"Hey, don't worry about it. I always say you have to be on the same level as the people you are working with to be effective. Take 'er easy, pal!"

Leo pushed his chair back. His beer glass was empty. "And it will stay empty," he thought.

He leaned back in his chair and ran his fingers through his hair again. The little doll beside him saw it and giggled. Someone laughing at him whether or not it was about his hair no longer bothered him. Maturity had taken away childish peeves. Leo just closed his eyes to help himself get a grip on the situation.

"If these kids are going to be educated on the hazards of drugs, it's not going to be by me. They've seen me drunk; what I would have to say would be sneered at. I'll mention this to Stan; maybe he can do something. Right now the best thing for me to do is to go home."

He left his chair to go to the washroom. Looking in the mirror showed him his unruly hair at its worst. Upon returning to the table a full glass of draft greeted him

"Hey, where did this come from?"

"Sit down, Pal, and have another. You're starting to get wound up like a clock. Sit and relax, the night is still young. Besides I bought it for you and I usually consider it an insult if a drink I buy is not drank"

Leo knew it was good policy to humor drunks, just as people humored him when he was on a tear. So he sat down and took a sip and did some more thinking.

Realizing that not a word of drug precaution had been said by the stranger/friend he inwardly moaned, "I've been taken! But why?"

By the time his glass was half drank, his usual love of young people was turning to dislike, even to hate. They were all laughing and talking at the same time, the noise was becoming unbearable. He wanted to slap them silly, to shut them up. Finally throwing his arms in the air he shouted "Shut up!"

They all turned to him to see him lower his hands to his head and pull on his hair. The 'doll' giggled and said, "Now you look like a lion!"

Something snapped inside Leo. He jumped up from his chair sending it flying. Grabbing her by the front of her shirt he stood her on her feet and gave her a quick shake.

IF ONLY...

A snap was heard. As light a sound as it made, in the minds of a bunch of potheads, the sound was magnified to outlandish proportions.

The silence was deafening as Leo, with stunned face and hammering heart slowly lowered her to the floor. Her head rolled back then sideways again when it came into contact with the dirty cafe carpet. Leo continued to hold her shirt unable to make any more moves as the awful deadly truth of what he had done began to sink into his fuddled brain.

Everyone had eyes only for the 'doll' on the floor. No one had seen the disappearance of Leo's newfound acquaintance.

CHAPTER 9

The story was in the newspaper the next morning. It was on page two about halfway down. Had this event happened in a small town it would have hit the front page and been the 'talk of the town' for weeks. But this was just big city news, just another slum crime, one of thousands that occurred during the course of a year. It didn't mention the name of the victim as she was a juvenile but it did mention the name of the criminal, the location and that it was drug related; not much more. It was enough to shake the heads of middle and upper class people. It was enough to nearly send Stan into shock when he read it.

Wearing the uniform of the city police, Stan had very little trouble getting in to see Leo. They were even given a private room. Stan checked for cameras and mikes before speaking.

"Leo, whatever happened?"

"I don't really know" Leo said in a voice of wonderment and despair. "I don't really know" he repeated with his head in his hands, elbows on the bare wooden table.

"Can you tell me anything?" Stan asked kindly.

"Yes and no. I don't know. It all happened so fast. But it wasn't me doing it, someone else had taken over my mind and body!"

IF ONLY...

"What do you mean?" inquired Stan.

Again Leo repeated, "I don't know. I can't think; I've had very little sleep. The cell they put me in was damn cold. The thin blanket they gave me didn't do a hell of a lot of good. Then there were questions, mug shots, and blood tests...Stan, that's what I can't completely understand. They found traces of LSD in my blood!"

Somehow Stan didn't really find this surprising. He felt that Leo, no matter how drunk he got on alcohol, would not go to the extremes he did unless there was "outside help", so to speak. But with Leo's vehement hatred of drugs, how did he come to have it in his blood stream?

Stan said, "Tell me the whole story, Leo. Don't leave anything out. I've got time to listen."

"I don't know where to start," Leo lamented, his head still between his hands. He sat quietly for a moment. Stan patiently waited while he sat at the other end of the table. Soon Leo lowered his arms and clasped his hands in front of him and said, "I guess I'll start by saying I've been fighting off a binge for quite sometime. You know my mother drinks and in that way I am her son. You know how I struggle with that problem because I can see what's become of her. I can't go to her for help. I only have one friend and that's you."

"And that's why I'm here, Leo. But go on with your story." Leo didn't seem to hear what Stan said. He continued in the same vein. "Lisa's picture sometimes helps but...." Leo stopped talking. His gaze became far away as his mind conjured up the framed picture of Lisa that stood on his night table. But Lisa's hair was not strawberry blonde; her eyes were not hazel. Instead a blue-eyed blonde posed in the frame.

Stan saw the look. He reached for Leo. "Leo, what's wrong? You okay?"

Stan's touch and voice brought Leo back to the present. "Yeah. Yeah, I guess I'm alright." He said while shaking his head.

Resuming his former position Stan encouraged Leo to tell his story. "That's the only way I can help you" Stan concluded.

"Yeah, I guess so" Leo sighed a heavy sigh, pulled himself together and began.

He told of going to the bar with the intentions of having only a few. Meeting this fellow who seemed against drugs as much as Leo was changed the whole scenario.

"He seemed so enthusiastic about drug prevention that I got excited over the fact that maybe we have another drug fighter. I didn't realize how much I was drinking. For that matter, how much both of us were drinking. I didn't stop to think that if we're going to meet these young kids we shouldn't be drunk when we get there. I didn't think of that until later at the cafe. It was then I realized that this guy hadn't said a word about drug prevention. At that time I didn't ask why but as I think of it I wonder if it was because he realized how drunk he was and how useless it would have been to speak to them at that time. I now wonder if he was supplying them with weed. When I realized this was not a good scene I noticed that most of them were acting happier more than in a normal way. I finished my beer and said to my self this is nuts! We'll not go any where in this situation!"

"After returning from the washroom, there was another mug of beer at my place. I didn't want it. I wanted to get out of there. I wanted to get my thoughts straightened out. But he insisted so I drank it thinking I'll just leave after this one. I really don't know how much of that mug I drank but my whole world seemed to change. Their laughter seemed to echo in my head, to drown out any sensible or stupid thought I had. I don't really remember what happened after that until everything went quiet. When I laid her on the floor I had the uncanny feeling that she was dead!"

Leo stopped talking. Momentarily he raised his clasped hands to his forehead. Stan noticed Leo's shaking shoulders and knew that the stress of all that had happened was finally getting to Leo.

Stan went to Leo putting his own arm around Leo's hunched shoulders. Through sobs, Leo burst out "Stan, I killed her. I killed somebody's daughter. A daughter who was loved as I would have loved a daughter of my own."

A lump in Stan's throat prevented him from saying anything. Finally he croaked out "I know how you wanted a family, Leo, I know. But though it's good to think of others, you are going to have to keep yourself in control, think of yourself and how you are going to get out of this mess. I'll help you as much as I can but you have to co-operate. Now, what was this guy's name?"

"I don't know," Leo said shaking his head on his clasped hands.

"What did he look like?" Stan asked.

Leo shrugged his shoulders. "Just an ordinary 'Joe Blow' Nothing special about him…"

Stan sighed, "Well, Leo, you haven't given me much to go on and yet you have. See ya, later." He gave Leo a gentle slap on the shoulders.

As Stan reached the door, Leo called out 'Stan!

Stan turned "Yes, Leo?"

"If I ever get out of this mess I'll never drink a drop of alcohol in my life. I mean that!"

"That's good to hear, Leo. I've already made that same promise to myself. Thanks, Leo."

"Thanks, Stan."

It wasn't long after Stan's visit Leo was escorted to the visitor's room, to a chair in a cubicle having a metal mesh glass partition separating the visitor from the criminal. As he sat down he took in his visitor—a small thin woman with short dyed orangey-red spiked hair. Slender crossed legs were topped with a mini skirt.

A pair of hands was clasped on top of a purse whose shoulder strap hung loose on her sweatered shoulder. When he took a good look at her pixie face he suddenly jumped from his chair, his hands went forward to grab her shoulders but flattened out on the glass instead.

"Lisa" he cried as the policeman sat him, not too gently back in his chair.

"Lisa!" he repeated. "What are you doing here?" His eyes were wide with wonderment, astonishment and with gladness.

Her soft voice he remembered so well said "I saw your name in the paper. I had to come to see if that name belonged to a man I once loved very much, to whom I gave my life, then to have him walk out on me."

Leo cringed at the accusation although he was glad to hear her confession of love. Clasping his hands he placed them between his knees lowering his head between hunched shoulders.

Her voice became husky. "Why did you do it, Leo?"

Raising his head he looked into her eyes. Through the heavy makeup he could see by their swollenness that she had been previously crying very hard. Thinking those tears had been for him he felt ashamed yet glad. Mixed emotions ran through him. He wanted to explain but how could he without hurting her more. Putting one hand on the shelf of the cubicle he opened his mouth to speak.

"No, Leo" Lisa said as she uncrossed her legs to slide to the edge of her chair. She placed both hands on her side of the shelf, her purse falling to the floor but catching by the strap in the crook of her arm.

"No, Leo" she repeated. "Let me talk. I need to find some answers. I need to know why you left me behind to look after our baby alone, to see our daughter's first steps by myself, to hear her first words by myself, to comfort her by myself when her grandfather's diabetes finally took his life. These are home things you talked so much about and you threw them away. Why?"

She didn't wait for an answer. "Once Dad was gone I was left alone to support her by myself in the only way I was capable of and that was to degrade myself on "the streets."

Tears were beginning to make a mess of her makeup giving her the appearance of someone from a horror movie. Indeed, to Leo, she was unraveling a story more terrible than any scriptwriter could think of.

Oblivious of the spectacle he was making of herself she continued to turn the man she was speaking to into an icy stone figure. Each word confirmed to Leo what a complete dunce, what a complete ass he had made of himself and those he loved. But worst was yet to come.

"I'd leave after Stacey was sleeping but there were many times I returned in the early hours of morning to find her on the floor or on the couch with swollen eyes and a tear stained face. I would pick her up and hold her so close to me and cry "Leo, where are you?"

Once she started school I tried waitressing in the daytime but I still had to leave sometimes at night. As she grew into a teenager I'd come home to find her gone. Where I don't know. She never told me. But now, Leo, thanks to you, I know where she is!"

Too many things were adding up too fast. It wasn't going to be pleasant but he had to know "Where is she?" he croaked.

"In the police morgue" was barely an audible answer.

With a face as white as new snow he uttered "Why?"

By this time Lisa's nerves were strung tighter than a guitar string. She was shaking visibly. Finally the guitar string broke. She screamed, "Because some goddamned drunken fool killed her!"

No longer able to control herself she jumped up and started beating with clenched fists on the glass partition yelling, "Leo, you killed our daughter!"

CHAPTER 10

Stan didn't waste any time in his search for Leo's freedom. He went straight to the morgue to find out the name of the victim. Maybe through her parents or friends he could find out whom she had been hanging out with.

As he made his way down the long familiar corridors to the morgue, he debated on how much he should tell Leo. If someone else put some grass into Leo's beer that person would be the "accessory before the fact" in regards to the crime. Stan felt Leo's stranger "friend" was responsible for the LSD but he had to prove it. Why this guy wanted Leo out of the way, Stan was unsure of. However, he was sure neither of them had contemplated murder.

Stan was also sure that if by chance, luck or good detective work he did find this creep, the creep was not going to be stupid enough to fink on anyone else especially not himself. And especially since his "Let's see what happens if…" game turned into a homicide in which he was deeply involved come hell or high water!

As Stan was not an uncommon figure in the morgue he had no trouble in obtaining the particulars of last nights juvenile victim. He

IF ONLY...

noticed she was about fifteen years old, had blue eyes, blonde hair, just barely five foot tall. Her name was Stacey...!

Stacey what? No. No, not possible. There are so many, many people with this same last name. But the description, the age, seemed to fit.

"Could...uh...could I see this corpse? He fearfully asked.

More red tape followed but soon he was looking down into a small very familiar pixie face. The hair was disheveled but the part could readily be noticed as being in the middle. Had it been redder, and he could have sworn the eyes should have been hazel. Time flooded his memory confirming that this indeed was Lisa's daughter.

His feet dragged his numb body as he retraced his steps. Did Leo know? Has Lisa been notified? Both these questions were assumedly answered when he entered the main precinct area just in time to see a policewoman escort a weeping, half hysterical pixie faced bundle of skin and bone into the back seat of a police car. They no doubt were taking her home. Hopefully there would be someone to stay with her.

As always in a crisis, Stan's brain clicked into gear. A few phone calls provided a home care nurse for a week or so for Lisa; the funeral and burial were taken care of financially and a lawyer obtained.

Now to see to Leo's condition.

Leo heard pounding long before Lisa's fists hit the glass partition. The word "diabetes" pounded the loudest. Then there was "daughter." "degrade myself" followed by the most brutal "killed."

A cloud of doom of the blackest color descended down upon him. So thick it was that it shut out the police woman taking Lisa away, the police man guiding him to a back room where even the lights were darkened by this cloud.

Leo was unaware of the length of time it took for the friendly and concerned voices to penetrate the pounding in his brain. As the darkness receded it allowed him to make out the burly, comforting form of his best buddy, Stan. Consciousness of his surroundings brought on the shakes, which brought on a shot in the arm. Some control came a few minutes later.

Oblivious of the police medics and guards he spoke to Stan in a voice of disbelief.

"Stan, I killed my daughter!" As the awful truth took hold he sobbed, "Stan, I killed my own daughter!" Burying his face in his hands, his elbows on his knees, he cried harder than he ever did before in his life: even more than on the night his daughter was conceived.

Compassion is rarely shown in the world of law and order but Leo's case was so pathetic that the sergeant of the precinct allowed Stan to accompany Leo back to his cell and also to stay with him. Maybe it wasn't compassion shown, but economics practiced. He wouldn't have to pay Stan to keep an eye on Leo—who definitely needed watching—like he would a medic.

Whatever the reason it was long after midnight when Stan was driving the still busy streets of the city towards his own sanctuary.

Turning into his driveway he pushed the button for the automatic garage door opener. He drove in, shut off the ignition, the garage door closed behind him. Folding his arms on the steering wheel and laying his head on his arms he thought "This has been a long day, a very, very long day. As long as life itself!" He rolled his head from side to side still hearing Leo's voice blaming Lisa in one breath while in the next chiding himself for being so stupid and thoughtless.

"Why didn't she tell me she lived with her father who was a diabetic?" He sat on the cot but only for a second. Standing and pacing the floor words like "But why didn't I ask about her family?" came from his mouth. Justification for him came "But I didn't want to be nosey!" The self-argument came back "But wasn't I planning to be part of her family. I had every right to know what I was getting into!"

This went on all evening and into the night until finally the four-hour repeats of sedatives took hold of Leo's hypoactive body. Succumbing to the medical drug he took his argument into the land of the deep sleep of exhaustion.

Stan slowly climbed the stairs to his bedroom, quietly undressed and slipped in beside his sleeping wife, taking her in his arms. His last thought, as usual, was of her. 'She seems to be slimming down a bit. Maybe it's just my imagination after seeing Lisa's thin frame."

It's immaterial to Leo's story to state the details of Leo's court days, of the arguments for and against. Leo pleaded guilty and stuck to his plea even though he realized that he did the dastardly deed under the influence of an unnatural substance. His own argument was that if he hadn't have been drinking there would not have been a device provided for the drug. The argument was the same if he had only been smoking—the cigarette offered a place for an illegal substance. So when the judge sentenced him to one year for manslaughter he took his punishment willingly.

The year went fairly fast. Periodically Leo was called to the identification room to survey suspects behind a two-way window. His inability to identify his so-called friend could be attributed to either the fact they had not found the culprit or to the fact that Leo continued to feel the crime fell squarely on his shoulders and his shoulders only—the reason having been given above.

Whether or not the drug dealer was ever found is not known. There were many who skipped town when the place got too hot to handle.

There were many found stabbed in alleys, washed up on the riverbank or heavily mutilated beside the train track. Having no positive identification of Leo's friend, anyone of these could have been him.

Lisa came every Sunday afternoon. She kept repeating, "At least I know where she is and I know where you are, too." Leo read this statement as a very important one to Lisa. He started to realize how alone she must have felt for the last fifteen years with no one to comfort or encourage her. This confirmed to Leo he was right in trying not to avoid his punishment. It wouldn't bring Stacey back but he felt he was doing something for his daughter, the child he had always wanted, the child he found, the child he threw away.

Even Christmas wasn't so bad. The inmates had a big turkey dinner; a Christmas tree was decorated and stood in the common room. Lisa came in the afternoon and Stan came in the evening with the good grace not to mention the joyous day he had spent with his family.

Stan's visits were sporadic due to his work and his family. Leo understood, relishing the thought that Stan was still standing by him. Noticing Stan's increasing worried and troubled face, Leo felt guilty of Stan's devotion to him.

On the day of Leo's release, Stan's devotion prevailed. They went for lunch together then to Leo's apartment, which, with Stan's help, Leo was able to hang on to. Again Leo thanked Stan profusely for all he had done and emphasized, "If there is anything—anything—in this world I can do for you please let me know."

They gave each other slaps on the back through a gripping handshake. Leo noticed Stan's eyes reddening as Stan made a sudden quick exit. "I never in my whole life thought that I would become the best of buddies with the bully!" was Leo's thought as he gently closed the door.

CHAPTER 11

Leo's vow to Stan to help him whenever came sooner than expected.

Tragic events generally have something good come out of them.

It was no different with Leo's unfortunate incident. Hashing over the proceeding events that led to Stacey's untimely death, the two "would-be heroes" of the drug prevention program realized just how vulnerable they were especially when they both had habits that invited drug abuse. Humbling themselves to the level of servitude they made an honest and successful attempt to rid them of anything that would hinder the procedure of eliminating or at least the prospect of eliminating the use of drugs by young or old.

When moving back into his old stomping grounds—in order to be closer to Lisa—Leo threw out all his ashtrays. Not wanting to be an alcoholic like his mother especially in his old neighborhood—pride stepping in here—Leo felt he would be able to kick his drinking habit quite readily.

He wasn't sure how well he could convince an old dog to do some new tricks but the thought had passed by his mind that maybe just maybe he or his colleagues could be of some help to his mother. Time would only tell.

He moved into an old brownstone again on the next street over from his old home where his mother still lived out a meager existence and where Lisa's cold water flat could readily be seen—a reminder he didn't need. He couldn't see the whole of St. Mathews church, the church he had wanted to marry Lisa in with hopes she would want that too, only a bit of the steeple, but he was able to hear the tingling sounds of the bells calling all to morning worship. The treed and spreading green lawn of the churchyard surrounding the church called to him each Sunday afternoon to come and visit the newest of graves. The short walk there enabled him—rain, sleet or shine—to answer that call.

Here it was that he settled down to a simple life. He was able to obtain employment at the old store—newly renovated under new management—where he first started out. They wanted to put him in a responsible position but Leo declined. A 9-5 job was all he wanted so as to devote his spare time to his pet project.

Here it was also that Lisa came to visit on her way home from waitressing at the corner cafe. Sometimes she would stay the night, well, not quite the whole night. After saying their good-nights, Lisa would turn her back to Leo wanting no more to do with him. When he awoke in the morning he would find her gone. He often wished he could wake to the sounds of her making breakfast but that was not to be. Sadly he accepted the fact that her nights on the streets accounted for her actions.

Here, again, it was that Stan would pick him up to take him to their drug prevention meetings. On an evening of an unscheduled meeting, Leo was surprised to find Stan on his doorstep.

Words were not needed to tell Leo that Stan needed help.

"What can I do for you, Stan?" Leo inquired as he held the door open invitingly wide.

Stan came in trying to keep himself together as Leo closed the door. He had trouble speaking. "I need you...!" He started again. "I need you to be a pallbearer for my wife. She passed away this morning of cancer!"

IF ONLY...

Leo immediately remembered the reddened eyes of Stan when Leo offered his help the day he was released from prison. Stan knew then that he was going to need someone soon and was glad he was going to be able to count on Leo.

Life and death go together. But when death stops by the wayside, life goes on. Stan's two kids went their own way and so did Stan. He sold the house and also moved back into the old neighborhood. His home, however, was not a brownstone; he had had enough as a kid. His preference of a higher standard of living showed through his humbleness to be close to the drug problem. His apartment was one of the newer ones about eight blocks away. Nonetheless he joined Leo each Friday night at the old still vacant lot to coach his makeshift team of basketball players in the ways and means of winning against Leo's makeshift team. The friendly competition made for some wild and noisy games.

The love and respect the kids had for these two middle-aged, overgrown kids spread to other neighborhoods. Soon Leo and Stan had quite a following of young people accounting for other activities to take place. The basketball coaches soon began to coach in the drug use and while not all listened, many did.

The "big kids" as Stan and Leo became known became a big part in the lives of that particular slum area of the big city. The years rolled by seemingly without a care until one day.

Lisa stopped by at Leo's one day after work but knocked on the door first rather than walking right in with a friendly "hello" as was her habit. Leo opened the door. Immediately Lisa anxiously asked "Have you seen Stacey? She's not at home!"

A cold chill swept over Leo. His mind and body became numb. A whispered "No!" was all he could mutter.

"Oh!" Lisa looked crestfallen but soon came alive. "Well, thanks anyway" and she was gone.

Still waters run deep so they say. Leo was disturbed at the ripple that was developing in Lisa's quiet life. Inconspicuously she needed to be watched.

Lisa never asked again where Stacy was but she did talk more about her than she had before. Leo felt that was a good sign relaxing his vigilance putting his mind to work elsewhere.

So on a Saturday morning as he walked on his way to the store he was shook out of his revere by the sounds of bottles being haphazardly clinked together. He took his eyes from the sidewalk to see an aging woman ahead of him pushing a grocery cart full of bottles.

"It can't be!" But it was.

He skipped down the alley to the back door of the store as he did in days of yore. He quickly went to the front windows just in time to see Lisa go into the bottle depot next door.

Hiding behind shelves he watched as she shopped spending only the few dollars she received from the bottles. The grocery cart carried the small bag back to her flat.

Leo was troubled. Was her pay at the cafe that poor that she had to resort to bottle picking again? It didn't make sense. He paid her rent so she would have plenty for food, utilities, and very few necessities and luxuries Lisa spent on herself.

Unsure of what to do he waited till the middle of the week to make a visit to her.

Rarely did he enter her apartment or for that matter that street. Guilt continued to plague him on the utter stupidity of his naïve, and thoughtless and young life.

He found her counting bottles into different price categories.

Not wanting her to know how disturbed he was, he cheerfully commented, "Is the bottle business doing well these days?"

She answered in an equally cheerful but serious manner. "Oh, yes! Those people who drink down by the railroad tracks are being so kind to me. There's always a plentiful supply. Daddy and I don't eat much so the bottles provide enough cash for groceries. I don't know how I'll pay the rent when he's gone. Thank goodness the welfare pays for his syringes and medicine!"

At the mention of syringes Leo took a quick look around. A box of needles "blazed" like a light on the counter. Where did she get them? Were they left over from years before? Wherever they came from, Leo knew somehow he had to dispose of them soon, very soon. Today's visit confirmed his worst fears. Lisa's mind was going. She could really harm herself if events were left to her.

He made his excuses and left miraculously with the needles. Immediately he called Stan. Stan came as quick as he could. They spent the evening discussing what and when something should be done.

After many days of scheming as to how to get Lisa to a doctor and after many doctors" visits, there was nothing else left to do but place Lisa in a home. To Leo's relieve she went gladly and cheerfully. During his weekly visits she repeatedly assured him she was quite happy there.

"I'm treated just like a queen! I don't have to cook or make my bed or wash the floors. On warm days I sit outside, And oh, Leo, the flowers are so pretty! They're just as pretty in Stacey's garden too. Oh, I didn't tell you. These lovely people found Stacey for me. She lives in paradise and has pretty flowers all around her all the time. Isn't that wonderful! I miss her but I'm glad she has a nice place to live."

Mixed emotions always filled the heart of Leo after these weekly visits. Thankfully Stan was always around to bring him back to normal. He sometimes wondered what "normal" was!

It was becoming quite a chore for Leo to walk the few blocks over to the vacant lot for the Friday night basketball games. He wasn't sure whether it was the personality of the kids participating or the mediocre enthusiasm of the younger coaches that made these nights not quite as exciting as when he and Stan were coaches. Neither was he sure how well these kids listened to him when he cautioned them about the use of drugs.

There were evenings when he dragged his feet through the falling dusk to sit on his steps—his sanctuary—to ponder on whether or not any of his teachings had done any good. Looking at his certificates of merit—the same ones hung on Stan's wall—from the drug prevention associations, from local churches, fire halls where he and Stan fought against drug abuse, brought him some satisfaction. But where were the certificates of merit from kids who either kicked the habit or heeded his warning. Just a nice thank you note would have been like a drink of water to a dying man. Faith in his own ability to teach against drugs was all he could hang onto. When he looked in the mirror to see an old white haired man, a man with hair so short he looked bald. Ever since that fateful day so many years ago (Just how long ago was it?) he never let his hair grow more than a half-inch long. He knew his teaching days soon would be ending. His only hope was that the younger replacements would do well enough to have certificates of merit on their walls too.

The ages of the people who lived in the old brownstone apartments ranged from newborns to very old. Sometimes there were more kids than adults; other times it was the other way around. Such was the case at the time of Leo's existence. It was not an uncommon sight to see an ambulance drive through the streets after having taken a deceased Grandma or Grandpa to be prepared for their final resting place. A few days later the bells of St. Mathews would ring announcing the occasion of the dear departed soul.

Leo knew that it wouldn't be long before the bells would be ringing for Stan and himself. He wondered if Lisa would understand when they told her he had passed away.

Stan had difficulties getting his heavy-set body around. Gout caused by his days on the beat hampered his movements. Frequent calls on the phone kept him in close contact with Leo. The odd time one of his grandchildren would drive him over to his best buddies for a most pleasant afternoon of memories, current events and future plans.

Preparing for each other's funerals was the biggest plan for the future. Leo had asked Stan to be his and Lisa's executor. If Stan were to go first, his son would look after all three. Knowing all was in place for the future was a secure comfort, leaving memories and current events as prevalent topics at their afternoon get-togethers.

One hot summer afternoon when the flies were buzzing in the gutters, and the heavyset lady in the apartment next to Leo's was trying to cool her shift-dress clad body by using the fan sitting in the open window, there came an ambulance up Leo's street. It stopped in front of Leo's brownstone, where the paramedics entered the apartment next to the heavyset lady's. They removed a body wrapped in a white sheet, taking it to a place for preparation. A few days later a heavy set man visibly suffering from gout, came to the empty apartment removing only certificates of merit from the walls. And, oh yes an old battered basketball. A call to the Salvation Army took care of the rest of the deceased's belongings.

Four days later Stan found himself the chief mourner for the third time in his life. The church was packed. Looking around he felt - not in a selfish or arrogant way – confident that he was looking at the preview of his own funeral to come. Such was the popularity of these two old cronies.

As they lowered the casket into the ground beside a small headstone marked only with 'Stacey", the date of her birth and the date of her death, visions came back to him of Lisa beside him not shedding a tear but standing stone faced and rigid. Did she ever cry over her great loss? Or is that the reason why she was in the home? He wondered when he would be chief mourner again, if ever!

Lisa was sitting out on the deck of the home enjoying the sunshine when, she suddenly stood up and said "Oh! The bells of St. Mathews are ringing, that means I've got to go and lay down. I'll soon be meeting Leo and Stacey. I need my rest!"

The majority of the people residing in that home were mentally handicapped. However, the staff could attest to the fact they had very good hearing. If any of them had been asked how long the bells of St. Mathews rang, they would have asked "What bells, we didn't hear any bells ringing!" The staff would confirm, "We are too far away to hear the bells of St. Mathews!"

Her slippered feet shuffled down the hallway to her room. She laid her thin body down on top of her bed, crossed her hands on her chest and went to sleep.

At that moment, Stan felt a cool breeze pass across his shoulders chilling him. To others, the day was hot and stuffy. Then a swooshing noise whispered in his ear accented by the clear sounds of joyful laughter. Had he been a clairvoyant or a physic he would have been able to observe a thin wisp of cloud ascend into the sky as it carried three souls, well overdue in their reunion, out into space, out into oblivion.